I Was a 98-Pound Duckling

Yearling Books are designed especially to entertain and enlighten young people. The finest available books for children have been selected under the direction of Charles F. Reasoner, Professor of Elementary Education, New York University.

For a complete listing of all Yearling titles, write to Education Sales Department, Dell Publishing Co., Inc., 1 Dag Hammarskjold Plaza, New York, N.Y. 10017

I WAS A 98-POUND DUCKLING

Jean Van Leeuwen

A YEARLING BOOK

Published by
DELL PUBLISHING CO., INC.
1 Dag Hammarskjold Plaza
New York, N.Y. 10017

Yearling ® TM 913705, Dell Publishing Co., Inc.
ISBN: 0-440-44190-0
Reprinted by arrangement with The Dial Press.
Printed in the United States of America
Eighth Dell printing—January 1981
MPC
Cover illustration by Rosemary Wells

*For Lucie and Barbara
and especially Guy*

I Was a 98-Pound Duckling

It was funny the way it happened. Not like you would expect at all. But then, I have noticed that most things in life are like that. They're either a lot nicer than you ever expected or a lot more horrendous. And they never happen when you are waiting for them, absolutely never. In my experience, the most earthshaking things always happen while you are standing there looking the other way or filing your nails or sharpening a pencil, totally convinced that nothing is ever going to happen to you in your entire life.

(3

One

I was sitting cross-legged on my purple-and-orange striped beach towel drying my hair in the sun and thinking what a nuisance it was to have problem hair. I had only recently discovered that my hair had so many things wrong with it. For the first thirteen and a half years of my life I had gone along blissfully unaware that my plain old straight brown shoulder-length hair was actually a tangled nest of problems waiting to be solved by modern cosmetic science. Beth was the one who told me. It seems that hair as impossibly fine as mine needs several preparations to give it body and sheen and that silky look that men find irresistible. It's got to be treated with special protein-formula shampoo and comb-through conditioner to cure split ends and preferably a color-heightening rinse, and it must be brushed practically constantly to make it gleam. That's the only way you can get away with fine hair, according to the magazines. It's got to gleam.

Beth brought a ton of beauty magazines and a whole suitcase full of little vials and jars and tubes of things when she came to visit me at the lake, and we are going to make a study of our beauty problems and do something about them. Our Bible is the June issue of *Allure* magazine, which is devoted to creating "A New Summer Beautygirl: You." I hardly know where to start, my beauty problems are so many and varied. But Beth is doing pretty well at mastering hers. She has only been here three days and already has a date with a boy she met at the beach. Of course, she doesn't have my hair problems. Hers is coarse and naturally curly and the magazines say the only hope is to wear it short and wash it all the time. Either that or have it straightened, and her mother won't let her. She has just finished washing it and already it is dry enough to go out on a date.

She banged out the kitchen door of the cabin.

"How do I look, Kath?"

She was wearing her new navy bell-bottoms and a red-and-white knit top, and her figure was still almost as pudgy as it was when I first met her in second grade, but she looked pretty too. Beth has what my mother once called "the face of a china doll"—high cheekbones and pale-pink clear skin which is absolutely immune to pimples and other skin disasters. When we graduated from eighth grade in June it was recorded in our yearbook that the composite "ideal girl" had "Beth Hardy's complexion." The ideal girl did not have my anything.

"You look great," I told her. "That new conditioner really helped, I think."

"If only I don't split my seams getting into the boat," Beth said. "I'd just die. I bet I've gained five pounds since I've been here."

Now I haven't seen Beth eat more than a sparrow's portion of anything since she's been here, so I didn't think this was very likely. But she does put on weight easily, unlike me. I have never weighed more than ninety-eight pounds in my entire life and probably never will. I look like a concentration-camp victim, which is just another one of my beauty problems.

Tactfully changing the subject, I asked, "Where are you going in Jimmy's boat?"

"Oh, just around the lake," she answered. "He said he would show me around."

Beth has already seen the lake in our outboard, but I suppose it might look different in Jimmy Weston's zillion-horsepower inboard with the real-leather red upholstery. The Westons are quite well-off, according to my father, and I guess they must be to have a fancy boat like that plus two sailboats and a fleet of canoes. Plus they have a compound of houses for various branches of the family, just like the Kennedys. Jimmy Weston never said more than three words to me before Beth came to visit.

"Well, don't let him show you Lone Point," I warned her. Lone Point is a narrow point of land with a deserted old house on it that is a noted lovers' lane.

Beth nodded and just then my father called from the front porch, "Beth, there's someone approaching on a white horse to see you." That's my father's idea of humor.

Beth grabbed the mirror out of my hand and gave her hair a few last licks with her brush. "Have a good time," I said.

"*Tout à l'heure*," she replied, and strolled casually around to the front of the house. Cool, that's Beth. She has nerves of steel more becoming to a foreign agent than to a girl of her age.

I heard some polite three-way conversation from the porch and then the sound of Jimmy's convertible driving away. One nice thing about him, he's sixteen and has his license, but I personally don't think that makes up for everything. I have never thought Jimmy Weston was much. He's short and skinny and his ears stick out and he never talks to people. I maintain this is because he's a snob, but Beth says he's just shy. Maybe her date with him will reveal who is right.

A minute later my mother came to the kitchen door and said she and my father were going shopping in town for the weekend food and did I want to come. The nearest town with a supermarket is sixteen miles away, so shopping is a big deal and takes a couple of hours. I said no, I'd stay here. I figured I'd get a chance to work on my beauty problems in peace.

"Where's Lisa?" I asked.

"She's over at Nancy O'Brien's," said my mother.

"If we're not home by five, would you light the oven and put the casserole in?"

I said I would and my mother and father drove off and I was alone. It was a peculiar feeling being alone at the cabin. I practically never had been before. But it was kind of nice. There were all the usual sounds of kids splashing and mothers yelling for them not to go out too far and dogs barking and motorboats passing on the lake, but it all seemed far away even though the beach is just down the road. Behind the cabin there was only the sleepy hum of a bee browsing in the grass and tree leaves whispering together overhead. Every once in a while a chipmunk would dart up a tree out of the corner of my eye, but otherwise it was like the whole world was standing still.

The sun was hot and I could feel it drying my hair and maybe bleaching it to a more interesting color, although I doubted it. My sister Lisa's hair is dirty-blond in winter and honey-blond in summer, but mine is just mouse-brown all year round. I flipped through the July issue of *Beauty* to the column called "Dear Beauty Editor," to which people write for advice on their beauty problems. I've never written in about any of mine, but I always check to see if by any chance anyone who does write in happens to have the same beauty problems I do. I was in luck this time. There was a letter from a girl who was sixteen and six-foot-two and worried she was still growing. This happens to be one of my secret fears. I'm not six-foot-two yet, but I'm not sixteen either. I figure a couple of more years at my current rate of growth could get me there. I'm already taller than almost everyone of the opposite sex I know, with the exception of my father, whom everyone says I take after. He's six feet tall exactly, and it's a well-known fact that children of today tend to grow taller than their parents due to better nutrition, so I could easily pass him and become the first girl in history to play professional basketball. I worry about it quite a lot. Sometimes I think that if one more smart-mouthed boy passes me on the street and says wittily, "How's the weather up there, Shorty?" I will vomit.

The beauty editor replied that studies show that girls usually get their growth earlier than boys and to always be proud of your height and not hunch over and that all models are tall and to take comfort from the fact that tall girls can wear the bold, exciting fashions of today that short girls can't get away with. I didn't take too much comfort from any of this. I figured I would rather have a date with a boy I could look up to literally as well as figuratively than model the bold, exciting fashions of today. Besides, I could never become a model on account of all my other beauty problems. Even models are supposed to have a slight suggestion of what my mother calls "a figure," and I don't. Plus I have problem skin. It has stubbornly resisted a whole medicine cabinet full of soaps, salves, and ointments and the advice of countless articles in all the magazines. I've just about decided to give up and wait until I outgrow it, which should only take about five more years. To top everything off, I bite my nails. I have been doing it as long as I can remember, and my mother has been nagging me about it as long as I can remember, but I can't stop. It's like a strange compulsion or something. I don't even know I'm doing it.

I recently decided to break this repulsive habit, and this spring I went on a campaign to make my nails stronger and thus harder to bite. You do this by consuming vast quantities of gelatin, which is supposed to have magic nail-hardening properties. Every morning I mixed an envelope of gelatin with my orange juice, held my nose, and gulped it down. I had to give it up after a week, though, because while my nails were still weak, I had the distinct feeling that my insides were starting to gel.

I closed the magazine suddenly, feeling like a real mess. As a matter of fact, I have felt like a real mess for quite some time now. Like the original ugly duckling. And the impression I get from reading the magazines is that I would have to spend all my waking hours and ten times my allowance to do anything about it. I mean, I don't see how all those society ladies whom you see photographed attending those charity balls have time to do anything but sit around all day with their hair in rollers and their faces in moisturizing cream. Sometimes I wonder if it's worth it. Or if even modern cosmetic science can transform an ugly duckling into a swan. Maybe I'd be better off just to give up now and plan a career as a nun.

The truth of the matter is that I have never had a date. I have never even been asked out by a creep. No boy of any description has ever called me on the phone except to ask about the math homework. Well, there was one boy who called about the math homework who sounded as if he might be going to ask me for a date, but since he is a complete creep I told him my father was expecting a long-distance call and I had to get off the phone. That was Freddy Lipton, who happens to be the shyest boy who ever lived. My mother once advanced the theory that shy people are deep and sensitive and worthwhile ("Still waters run deep" was the quaint way she put it), so I resolved to get to know Freddy Lipton better. For a whole week I made it a point to talk to him in study hall, which was a strain since he turned bright pink whenever anyone spoke to him. But it turned out that Freddy Lipton was an exception to my mother's theory. Not only was he the shyest boy who ever lived, but the most boring. His idea of a good time, I found out, was to compute daily the batting averages of every single player on the Boston Red Sox. Every day he did it, except when the previous day's game was rained out or something. Then he did some other complicated calculations, predicting how their final averages would compare to last year's or something. One day in study hall, after I made the mistake of displaying polite interest, he put his arm over his paper so no one else could see and revealed to me his secret mathematical formula. *Quel* bore.

I guess I could have had a date with a creep if I had wanted to. But when you think about it, that's even more depressing. I mean, he must have thought I was a creep too.

Beth and I used to spend every Saturday night together. We would watch old movies on TV on her sun porch and gorge ourselves on cashew nuts and cut out pictures from *House Beautiful* of the houses we'd have someday. I was going to be an architect and she was going to be an interior decorator and we were going to be business partners. We designed our company stationery and everything. It was going to say: *McGruder and Hardy. Complete Home Design.* But in the last couple of months Beth has lost interest in interior decoration. She says she's not sure she wants to mix marriage and a career. It's not that she's against Women's Liberation or anything, it's just that she's not sure it's fair to a child to leave him all day in a day-care center. The reason for her change of heart is that two boys have asked her out. She's not in love with either of them, but she went out on six dates this spring. She even went to a dance at some country club, and her mother let her buy this terrific red dress with a bare midriff.

It never seemed depressing to watch old movies on TV at Beth's on a Saturday night, but it turns out to be very depressing when you watch them alone. Everyone I know has a boyfriend, even if he goes to another school and they just have a picture of him. Last year I had a picture of Dana in my wallet. He goes to Brown University, and I really only know him on a professional basis, so to speak. I took tennis lessons from him twice a week last summer. At the end of the summer I finally got up the nerve to ask if I could take his picture. I had this photograph of him standing at the net with his racket poised, and I used to show it to people and sort of imply that I'd gone out with him pretty frequently while we were at the lake. But then Marian Peretti started asking what he was majoring in and when he was coming to see me, and I started feeling bad about the whole thing and took his picture out. Now I just have pictures of my parents and Beth and Cricket, our dog who was put to sleep last year.

I stretched out flat on my back, removed a pine cone from under my spine, and closed my eyes. I tried to imagine what it would have been like to go out with Dana. He wasn't so good-looking—medium-tall and stringy with the kind of blond hair that always looked like he just got out of bed in a hurry and forgot to comb it—and he never said much except "Keep your eye on the ball now," but he had the nicest smile. Like he really understood things. That's what I think is important in a man. That and a sense of humor. And strong hands. Beth goes for broad shoulders, but I always look at a boy's hands. I can't stand skinny white hairy hands or fat freckly ones. Dana's hands looked like he could really build things with them. As a matter of fact, that's what he's doing this summer. His mother told my mother that he has a job out West somewhere building a road. Not by himself, of course, with a construction company.

I started fantasizing about how we would meet some day many years from now at a cocktail party in Manhattan. (I'm always having these fantasies, like for example if I'm carrying a book on a bus, I imagine that the author of the book is going to be on that bus and he'll see that I'm carrying his book and offer to autograph it for me. It hasn't happened yet, but it could. I always carry my books so you can see the titles, just in case.) My fantasy about Dana was that we'd meet at this party and he'd be a famous bridge-

(17

builder and I'd be a famous architect and we'd see right away that we had a lot in common. He wouldn't recognize me right away because I'd be wearing my hair piled on top of my head and have a large bust and be very sophisticated. Then I'd say something like, "You know, I think I've finally learned to keep my eye on the ball," and he'd look at me and suddenly begin to smile and say, "Kathy McGruder! Why the last time I saw you you were a skinny little kid with problem skin." And later on, after we were married, we'd laugh about it a lot.

I was just imagining the setting for this cocktail party, a penthouse on the fortieth floor with a magnificent view of the New York skyline, when I heard Lisa's giggle. I would recognize it anywhere. It proceeded up the road and onto the front porch and I heard her call, "Anyone home?" but I didn't answer. Nancy O'Brien was with her, and I could hear Lisa changing clothes in the bedroom and Nancy helping herself to the refrigerator and the *fffsst* of a flip-top can being opened. Then the porch door slammed again. Raising my head a fraction of an inch, I could see them walking barefoot down the road to the beach.

Walking barefoot always used to be one of my favorite things about summer. It was torture the first few days, but gradually I would toughen up my feet like an Indian brave so that by the end of the summer I could walk across a bed of hot coals practically and never feel the pain. But that was before I realized that my feet were one of my most grotesque features and should be covered at all times. Besides being the size of battleships, they have another peculiarity which I inherited from my father's side of the family. My second toe is longer than my big toe. My father and I may be the only two people in America who suffer from this affliction. It doesn't make so much difference for my father, but on a girl it's pretty revolting. I never knew before this summer how really hot sneakers can get.

Besides going barefoot, I used to like to do all sorts of outdoorsy things, like camping out overnight on the island across the lake and going hiking up Blue Mountain with my father and practicing tennis against the wall in the gym on rainy days in preparation for becoming a national champion. That was my last summer's fantasy. I was going to compete at Forest Hills. But now everything seems so complicated. I have acquired too many worries to enjoy life like I used to. So this summer I haven't done much of anything. Moping around, my mother calls it. I can see now what people mean when they say to enjoy your youth because it's the best time of your life. My youth has just fled.

Having a sister like Lisa has added to my already long list of worries. She is only a little over a year younger than me, and even though she is still really a child, boys are starting to notice her. I guess it's because of her long blond hair and this giggle that gets on your nerves when you live in the same house with her but which boys seem to find attractive. Also, even though we're related, she doesn't seem to have any of my beauty problems. Her toes are apparently inherited from my mother's side of the family, and she's neither too tall nor too short nor too fat nor too thin, which is very unusual among my friends. In fact, to be absolutely truthful, she is quite pretty. But don't get me wrong, I don't hate Lisa or anything. We've always gotten along pretty well considering we're sisters—I guess because we're so different that we don't have much to fight about. But the day before Beth came, Lisa and I and some other kids were fooling around out on the raft, pushing each other into the water and all that, and Tommy Whitaker, who is my age and cute but too short, started ducking Lisa and showing off his new backward dive, and all of a sudden I did hate Lisa. Just for a minute. I felt sick to my stomach and had to come out of the water, and I lay face down on my beach towel for about ten minutes trying not to cry.

I know how it's going to be with Lisa. She's going to have tons of dates. I don't know why, but I just know it.

I opened my eyes and stared up at the tops of the pine trees waving ever so slightly against the sky. And suddenly I had another one of my fantasies. It popped into my mind like a scene from a movie, complete with wide screen and glorious technicolor. The scene is Kennedy International Airport, and I am just descending the steps of a 747 and I am a famous reporter or maybe photographer for *Life* magazine returning from a dangerous assignment covering some war in Asia. And there, waiting to meet me, is Lisa. She's wearing a gorgeous fur coat and dripping with diamonds and looks like one of those models on the cover of *Vogue*, and with her is this tall blond football-player type and he's her husband. Holding onto their hands are two little kids, who are also blond and beautiful. And just

(*21*

as I get to the foot of the steps the kids come running toward me yelling, "Aunt Katherine! Aunt Katherine!"

That will be me. Aunt Katherine, the famous career woman.

Two

There is a square dance at the gym down the road every Saturday night. My parents are big on square dancing for some weird reason, and when I was little I thought it was great too, but now it seems pretty corny. There are two reasons to go anyway, however. The principal one is that there is nothing else to do around here on a Saturday night. The other is that the gym is actually two gyms, and the one that isn't used for square dancing is usually used for a basketball game by the boys who are working or visiting nearby.

I almost didn't go, I was feeling so depressed. But Beth talked me into it. Jimmy Weston was supposed to play basketball, and she had told him she would come and watch. I figured I would go and keep her company, and I could always come home early by myself if I felt like it. It was only a mile down the road. Besides, it seemed like a waste of clean hair to stay home by myself. Beth had combed through some conditioner after supper, and I thought I detected a slight improvement in my split ends.

The little kids were square dancing when we got there, and we stood around and watched for a few minutes. Little kids are fun to watch because they put so much energy into it and get all red in the face when they get mixed up, which is half the time. We could hear feet pounding and occasional shouts from the other gym so we knew there was a basketball game going on. Beth and I walked down the hall and stood in the doorway. Jimmy Weston didn't look over, but I knew he had seen us because he right away missed three easy baskets. We sat down on a bench near the door and I checked to see who was there. It was the usual Saturday-night crowd. Tommy Whitaker and

Jimmy Weston were the only two boys our age—the rest were older college guys. They didn't have real teams, but they chose up sides and then half of them would take off their shirts and the other half wouldn't and they called themselves Shirts and Skins.

A couple of the Skins were pretty repulsive looking, all hair and rolls of fat. Jimmy Weston was emaciated. The only one I thought was good-looking was Dave Dillon, and he's supposed to be practically engaged to a girl who waits on tables at a hotel down the lake. After watching the game for a few minutes I began to get bored. Basketball is a pretty dull game to watch, in my opinion. All they do is throw the ball around and yell and run from one end of the room to the other, and you can hear them panting and wheezing, especially the ones with the rolls of fat. And since the teams don't represent a school or anything, there's no one to root for unless, like Beth, you are partial to one of the players. Also, the smell of sweaty bodies gets pretty overpowering after a while.

Sitting where we were, there was the additional danger of being trampled to death by one of the players going out of bounds. After Tommy Whitaker almost landed in my lap, I told Beth I was going to get a drink of water and I left. I got a drink, checked my hair in the ladies' room, and then looked into the other gym. My parents were still watching the kids square dancing so I sat down on a bench with them. In a few minutes the kids' dancing was over, and my parents got up to form a square with their friends the Olivers and some other people.

"Want to be my partner for a set, Kathykins?" my father asked.

I shook my head. "I'll just watch," I said.

I sat on the bench with the Olivers' grandmother while the caller tried to get enough dancers to form another square. He got three couples but he couldn't get a fourth.

"How about one of you fellows grabbing a partner?" he called and I looked up and saw three boys I'd never seen before standing in the doorway.

They sort of ducked their heads and grinned and disappeared, and then the caller tried to get me and Miss Shelby, who is an old-maid schoolteacher of about fifty, to fill in the set. I said I was just leaving. I have made a firm resolution never to be the kind of person who dances with other women, even if I get to be a fifty-year-old old maid myself. So then the other three couples had to sit down, and the caller looked at me like it was all my fault, and I got up and left. For some reason, I felt like I was going to cry.

The basketball game was still going on, but I didn't want to go back in there so I went outside on the porch. I thought I would start walking home, but there was no one on the porch and it was nice and dark. I sat down in an old wicker rocking chair and looked up at the sky with millions of stars and a fat yellow moon lurking behind a tall pine tree and felt the breeze and heard the piano tinkling away inside and the caller calling, "Do-si-do your partner!" Somehow the combination of all this atmosphere was too much for me. It seemed like everyone in the world was paired off like in Noah's ark—everyone except Miss Shelby and me. A couple of tears spilled over and I could feel them rolling slowly down my cheeks, and then someone said, "Hi," and I gave a loud sniff and looked up.

There was a boy standing there. I couldn't see him too well, but right away he struck me as the best-looking boy I had ever seen. He was one of the ones who had been standing in the doorway watching the square dancing. And he was smiling at me.

"Hi," I said, hoping it was too dark for him to notice the tear marks on my cheeks. I wanted to sniff again but I decided I'd choke first.

"Are square dances a regular thing around here?" he asked. He had a nice voice, deep but quiet, with some sort of accent. He said *square* like it was *squayah*.

"Every Saturday night," I said. And then I couldn't think of anything else to say. All the magazine articles tell you to be gay and sparkling and witty when you meet a boy, and here was the most gorgeous boy I had ever laid eyes on, and my mind was a total vacuum. All those things I'd practiced saying in my mind in case the occasion ever arose just dribbled away like water down the drain.

He didn't seem to notice though. "I'm from Camp Wapanoc," he said. "That's on Hemlock Lake, about forty miles from here. It's just a pond compared to this lake. We're on a weekend canoe trip and we camped overnight on the beach here. We heard the music and came to take a look."

Over his shoulder I could see the other two boys in the doorway pretending to be watching the dancing but looking at us out of the corners of their eyes. Off through the trees I could make out what looked like a campfire. And now I could see that the white letters on his dark blue T-shirt spelled *Camp Wapanoc*.

"My name's Keith Bradley, by the way," he said.

Even his name sounded like an all-American hero, captain of the football team, member of the National Honor Society, and president of the Student Council.

"I'm Kathy McGruder."

"It's nice to meet you, Kathy."

Boys I knew never said things like that. Probably he helped little old ladies across the street too.

"Do you have a house near here?" he asked.

"Right down the road." I pointed in the general direction of our cabin. "We rent the same house for three weeks every summer. We've been coming here since I was two years old."

"It's a nice lake," said Keith. "I've been going to camp three summers. I'm a junior counselor this year."

"That's great," I said, smiling brightly. I remembered from the magazines that you're supposed to bubble over with interest in anything the boy is interested in.

"Well, you get a lot of frogs in your bunk, but it's O.K." He leaned back against the porch railing and smiled again, and my heart abruptly started thumping a mile a minute. He had the kind of smile that wasn't just pasted on his mouth, like a lot of people I know. It made you feel like it was just for you and nothing else in the world was on his mind at that moment. I could see his face better now, and he really was as good-looking as I'd first thought. He was at least as tall as my father and not too skinny and he had a wide mouth and a nice nose and curly dark hair that wasn't too long or too short but just nicely shaggy. Not like he spent hours on it, but like it just grew right. He was much better-looking than Dave Dillon. And I knew that if I didn't come up with a gay, sparkling, witty remark in about thirty seconds he would probably put out his hand and say, "Well, it was nice meeting you, Kathy," and walk right out of my life.

So I opened my mouth and what I said was, "Do you square dance?" I could have bitten off my tongue. It would have been better just to sit there like a bump on a log than to say a dumb thing like that. He'd think I was chasing him, which is the absolute worst thing a girl can do, according to the magazines.

He said, "Well, not exactly. At least I haven't tried it since I was about seven years old."

"Oh, I don't either," I said quickly. "It's really just for kids."

"I was kind of hoping they'd play a little rock after a while for a change of pace. But since that doesn't seem to be happening, why don't we try it? If you don't mind my tripping all over your feet, that is."

"Oh, I don't mind," I said. I stood up and my eyes came about to his chin. He must have been at least six-foot-two.

We stood in the doorway until the music stopped, and I was hoping the basketball game would be over and Beth would come out, but she didn't. I saw my mother glance over a couple of times, though, and she had this tiny little smile on her face.

I pointed out my parents to Keith.

"They look like they're having a good time," he said, and it was true. They always look that way when they square dance, as if they didn't have a care in the world, which I happen to know isn't true. It's the only time I've ever seen them hold hands, too. You wouldn't even know they were married.

When the music stopped, Keith said, "Come on, introduce me," and the next thing I knew he was shaking hands with my father and saying, "It's nice to meet you, sir." He smiled at my mother and said, "Your daughter has promised not to mind if I step on her feet." I could tell right away that my parents were impressed, which wasn't too hard to understand. It was probably the first time they had ever heard a boy say "sir."

He was a good dancer too. He only got mixed up

a couple of times and then he apologized all over the place and you could see everyone liked him. Mrs. Oliver was giggling and fluttering her eyelashes at him as he swung her around, which I personally thought was pretty sickening. For a minute it made me wonder if I could go for a boy who went out of his way to make adults like him like that, like maybe he was a phony. But then he came back to me and smiled that special smile into my eyes, and I decided he was just being polite and couldn't help it if Mrs. Oliver didn't act her age. And at the end of that dance he didn't drop my hand like he had before. We stood there holding hands right in front of everybody and it seemed natural and kind of inevitable, and his hand wasn't sweaty, either, which I always knew I would hate.

After the last dance we stood around with everybody for a couple of minutes, and while Keith was talking to my parents I saw Beth look in the door with Jimmy Weston. When she saw me holding hands with Keith I know she could have passed out, but with Beth no one would ever know. She doesn't lose her cool. She just waved and said, "We're going for ice cream. See you later."

I waved back just as cool, and Keith looked over to

see who I was waving at. "That's my friend Beth," I told him. "She's visiting me for a few days."

He turned back to my father and said, "I hope you don't mind, sir, if I walk Kathy home." My father gave me this long serious considering look, as if he was trying to make up his mind, and then he smiled and said that actually he didn't mind a bit.

He and Mom left in the car and Keith had to go tell the other two boys to go back to the beach without him. I went into the ladies' room to comb my hair, and while I was there I suddenly got this absolute conviction that when I came out he wouldn't be there. Probably he hadn't gone to tell the other boys at all but had just come to his senses and decided to make a getaway while there was still time. A boy as good-looking and smooth and tall as that could not possibly want to walk me home. It had to be a mistake. I could just see myself waiting and waiting for him and then walking home all alone down the dark road, weeping quietly—the woman abandoned, like in an old Bette Davis movie. And at the same time that I was afraid he wouldn't be there when I came out, I almost wished he wouldn't. It was a weird feeling, and my throat got very dry and my stomach felt like it had Mexican jumping beans inside of it. I just stood there holding onto the sink for a minute, and then I ran the water until it was icy cold and splashed it on my face. I stared at myself in the mirror. I looked so tragic that I had to smile, and then I was all right.

When I got outside, he really wasn't there. I started to get panicky all over again, but then I saw him in the shadows of the porch, leaning against the railing. Everyone else had gone home except the caller and his wife, who were packing up their music.

"Jack and Hotdog didn't understand why I wasn't going back with them," he said. "They're nice guys but a little bit slow in the head." He gave me that smile that seemed like it was just for me, and somehow everything seemed all right again.

"Hotdog?" I said. "What kind of a name is that?"

"It's his favorite food," said Keith. "He eats them for breakfast."

We walked down the dirt path under the pine trees, and after a minute he took my hand again, and it was very dark and the same fat moon and million stars were overhead but they looked different now. The only sound was the soft throbbing of grasshoppers in the field, so quiet that it was almost not a sound at all. We walked for a few minutes without saying anything, but this time I didn't care. I felt suddenly very small and fragile and protected with my hand enfolded in his big warm one, like someone who can't quite walk by herself. It was a whole new feeling. Then he asked me where I was from and I told him New Jersey and I found out he was from a small town outside Boston, which explained his accent, and that he went to a private school in New Hampshire and was fifteen but in the same class as me because he had to make up a year when he transferred to private school. And he was captain of the basketball team last year and went out for track and had placed first in the high jump in the meet between his school and their biggest rival.

I told him I liked sports too and all about the Y softball team I was on and how they made me play second base because I was the only one who could catch a ground ball, and then I remembered that being too interested in sports is not considered feminine, so I stopped in the middle of telling him about the playoffs we were in last spring and changed the subject.

We had just come to the spooky place in the road. That's what Lisa and I have always called it. Just before you get to our cabin there is a dip in the road and the woods are very thick on both sides and there aren't any houses. It's so dark that you actually can't see your hand in front of your face, and you think you're going to walk off the road any minute and wander in circles through the woods for hours. For years Lisa and I wouldn't walk home that way at night. Even with a flashlight it's spooky because the light makes long shadows that out of the corner of your eye look like vicious beasts about to leap out and devour you. Lisa was sure one time that she saw a bear, but my father took her back there in daylight and it turned out to be just a knobby old tree trunk. I started telling Keith about the time when I was about ten that Patsy Regan double-dared Lisa and me to walk home that way. Naturally we had to do it, and the three of us hung onto each other for dear life. Then all of a sudden we heard this rustling noise and Patsy yelled, "It's a snake!" and dropped the flashlight. She started to run and fell and skinned her knee, and there we were in the dark, feeling around for the flashlight with Patsy yelling her head off, "Snake! Snake!"

Keith laughed, and it seemed pretty funny now to me too. And somehow with him there holding my hand, the spooky place didn't seem as scary as it always had before.

In no time at all we were in front of the cabin. "This is it," I said. Our car was pulled up in front on the grass and there was a light in my parents' room and a small one in the living room that my mother must have left on for Beth and me. I couldn't tell if Beth was home yet or not.

We just stood there by the front steps not saying anything, but he didn't let go of my hand, and all of a sudden it occurred to me that maybe he was going to kiss me. And I was half hoping he would and half hoping he wouldn't because I'd never practiced what I'd do, not anticipating being in this situation in my entire life, and we'd probably bump noses or something horrendous like that.

But he didn't do anything. The moon was behind him so I couldn't quite see his face and I didn't know what he was thinking and the only sound was the grasshoppers, very loud now, as if they'd just been tuning up before. Finally I said, "I guess I'd better go in."

"Yeah, I guess so," he said. Then, like he'd just thought of it, he said, "We're not starting back until about three tomorrow afternoon. Would it be all right if I came over in the morning and we could go swimming or something?"

I couldn't believe he was saying it. I nodded.

"Is ten thirty too early?"

Beth and I have an ironclad rule that under no circumstances do we put a toe out of bed before eleven, but I said, "No, that's fine."

He still stood there not letting go of my hand, and he seemed different than he had before, not quite as supersmooth as I'd thought. Then finally he said, "Well, good night, Kathy."

"Good night," I said.

He was standing very close to me and he seemed to hesitate, and for a minute I stopped breathing, not knowing what was going to happen. But he just squeezed my hand once and let it go. I went up the steps to the porch very fast and just remembered to catch the screen door before it slammed.

When I looked back all I could see was a long shadow moving up the road and then he was swallowed up in the dark of the spooky place and was gone.

Three

I woke up early and for a minute I didn't know why.
I lay there looking up at where a beam of sun had
slipped through the curtains and made a yellow tri-
angle on the cardboard ceiling, and then I remembered. And the awful thing was it didn't seem real.
When I shut my eyes I could see myself walking down
a dark road holding hands with a boy, but it seemed
like a dream or a scene from a movie I'd seen a long

time ago. It had this vague, blurry quality. And when I tried to remember what he'd said and what I'd said, I couldn't. Here it was the most momentous event of my entire life, and I couldn't even remember.

I looked over at Beth's bed, but she was still asleep, curled up like a lump under the army blanket, facing the wall. She had come in last night right after I did, but I had pretended to be asleep. Somehow it had seemed then like the magic might wear off if I talked about it. Now that I wanted to talk, she'd undoubtedly sleep all morning. That's Beth. She is so calm she'll probably have to set her alarm to wake her up for her own wedding.

I couldn't just lie there so I got out of bed, trying not to squeak the springs too loud, took three long steps on the cold linoleum to the closet, crammed my feet into my sneakers, and tiptoed out. I thought for a minute that no one else was up, but my mother is always up early. She claims it is the best part of the day. I think that's because it's the only quiet time. My mother values peace and quiet a lot.

She was in the kitchen making sandwiches for a picnic lunch. "Well, good morning," she said. I noticed that she was wearing that same tiny little smile from last night.

For some reason it made me feel embarrassed. "Morning," I mumbled and went right to the refrigerator for some orange juice.

"He seemed like a nice boy," my mother said. She believes in coming right to the point.

"Mmmm," I said, striving for a noncommittal tone like Beth.

"Nice-looking too. And so tall. I told you if you waited a while you'd find the boys catching up to you."

"Mmm-hmmm," I said, drinking my juice with great concentration.

My mother finished putting lettuce in the sandwiches and started stuffing them into little plastic bags. "Up kind of early, aren't you?" she asked.

"Well," I said casually, "I have a date with Keith."

My mother's eyebrows went up about a mile and I couldn't help myself. I had to smile. "Oh, how nice," she said, and we sort of grinned at each other, and for a minute it was like we weren't mother and daughter at all but just friends.

Then she went back to being a mother and asked where we were going and who with. I said I really didn't know, but we couldn't go too far because he had to leave at three, and she said to be careful not to go far from shore in a canoe because they are tippy and dangerous. My mother has this great knack for anticipating disasters you would never conceive of in a hundred years. I said as far as I knew we weren't going canoeing, just swimming, and she said to be sure not to swim until an hour after lunch.

I changed the subject then and asked what the sandwiches were for.

"Oh, we're going to Indian Gorge with the O'Briens, don't you remember?"

Indian Gorge is this canyon with caves and waterfalls and supposedly Indian writing on the rocks. We went there once a few years ago. My parents have gone to all the places of historical interest for miles around, even the little dinky ones where some captain in the Revolutionary army fought some battle in the middle of a cornfield that nobody ever heard of. They really go for places of historical interest. It is my personal opinion, though, that these places are not all they're cracked up to be. What they usually consist of is some old rock or falling-down fort or log cabin, and next to it is a giant souvenir stand. And everyone buys a bumper sticker to show they've been there, and they take each other's pictures and throw candy wrappers all over the place of historical interest or carve their initials on it. I mean, the reason you go there is supposed to be to get the feel of what it was like to live a few hundred years ago, but I never can because of all the distractions from now. I was glad my parents were going, though, and especially with the O'Briens. I wasn't particularly anxious for Keith to encounter Lisa's blond hair and giggle.

I helped pack the lunch in the cooler, and then my father and Lisa were nagged out of bed by my mother and dragged to the breakfast table. As soon as Lisa woke up, which was about halfway through her corn flakes, she started asking me all kinds of questions about Keith. I was very cool in my replies but managed to slip in a mention of his winning first place in the high jump and being captain of the basketball team.

"I thought you said basketball was the most boring sport in the world," Lisa said, looking at my father and mustering up her first giggle of the morning. She has always been a tattletale and a blabbermouth.

I gave her a withering look, and my father ignored Lisa and said, "Nice boy. Very polite," and gave me one of his long serious looks that turned into a smile.

My father is kind of a quiet type, but he usually manages to come through with remarks like this when you need them most.

Lisa was practically hysterical because they had to leave for Indian Gorge before Keith was scheduled to arrive, but my mother said it was a long drive and they had to get started. Finally they got everything in the car and my mother leaned out and said, "Have a good time, dear," and they drove off about nine fifteen.

I went to the refrigerator and finished off some chocolate pudding, a glass of tomato juice, and a chicken leg and then tried to read a magazine. After about two minutes I couldn't stand it anymore, and I went in and woke Beth up.

"What time is it?" she mumbled. She sat straight up, looked at the clock with one half-open eye, and fell over again with the covers over her head.

"Beth, you've got to get up," I told her.

"Why? Do we have school?"

"No, I have a date."

That got her. She sat up again and her eyes were wide open this time. She looked like Little Red Riding Hood's grandmother in this crazy flowered hat that she wears to bed to keep her hair from standing on end.

"With that cool guy from last night?" she asked.
I nodded.

"*Fantastique!*"

"You've got to help me get ready," I said.

But Beth was already out of bed and running the water in the bathroom. "How did you meet him? Where is he from?" she asked through her toothbrush.

I told her about Keith while she ate breakfast, which for Beth consists of a glass of orange juice followed by several heaping spoonfuls of cottage cheese. Ever since Beth was discovered by boys she has been on a cottage-cheese kick. She eats it for breakfast, lunch, and dinner, over the protests of her mother, who fears for her life because she is not getting a balanced diet. Beth is trying to lose fifteen pounds and become svelte and sexy. On her cottage-cheese diet she has succeeded in losing a lot of weight, but unfortunately she has one fatal weakness. It is chocolate marshmallow sundaes. Every time she loses five pounds she decides she deserves a chocolate marshmallow sundae, and then she goes berserk and has about twelve of them and gains back the five pounds. She must have lost the exact same five pounds twenty times in the last six months. It is an unending cycle. If

I were her mother, though, I would buy cottage cheese by the truckload. While Beth was spooning it in and looking like she'd just discovered Howard Johnson's twenty-ninth flavor, I had another English muffin with strawberry jam. When I'm nervous I tend to eat without stopping.

I finished my account of last night, and I could tell Beth was impressed. She said she thought Keith looked like Harvey Goodman, which from Beth is the ultimate compliment. Harvey Goodman is this guy who lives across the street from her and goes to Harvard. Beth has had a crush on him since she was in the sixth grade. Not only is he poetry editor of the literary magazine, but he led a sit-in at the administration building last spring and spent a night in jail. He has dark curly hair that tends to stick up on end and brooding, tragic eyes and wears granny glasses. Recently he added a straggly little mustache which in my opinion makes him look like a rat. But Beth thinks he is gorgeous.

I thought Keith was infinitely better-looking myself, but I didn't want to make a thing of it. As soon as she put the top back on the cottage cheese I dragged her into the bedroom so we could get started on my hair. There was a style in the June issue of *Glamour* that she'd been practicing on me, and I wanted her to fix it that way today. As soon as my hair smelled the water it would fall apart, naturally, but at least it might look presentable for the first ten minutes.

"Where are you going on your date?" Beth asked as she got out the electric rollers.

I was peering into the mirror to see if my complexion was going to hold up or if I was about to erupt in a thousand pimples. Beth's mirror is one of those magnifying ones that makes each pore look the size of a moon crater. My chin was a disaster area, but otherwise the prognosis didn't look too bad.

"He said we'd go swimming or something," I said.

Beth selected a fat roller and started winding up my hair. "Why don't you go water-skiing with Jimmy and me?" she suggested. "He's coming to pick me up around eleven and we're going skiing from his dock."

It sounded like a good idea to me. Just going swimming at the beach with all the mothers and little kids was not what you'd call exciting, and Keith was probably a good water-skier, being an athlete and all. Besides, I was beginning to get this nervous twitch in the depths of my stomach, and it suddenly seemed really essential to have Beth there.

"I'll ask him when he comes," I said, and then I realized that I hadn't asked Beth a single thing about her date with Jimmy Weston, and she must like him because she'd gone out with him twice in one day yesterday and had another date with him today.

"Did you have a good time last night?" I asked.

"Ummm-hmmm," she said. "The Skins won, 48 to 32 or something like that, and then we went to that dairy place afterward. Jimmy had some kind of strawberry thing with a mountain of whipped cream, and I had a diet root beer."

I couldn't see her face because she was working on the back of my head, but I thought I detected a certain lack of cool in her voice.

"Do you like him better than Ted Hollaway?" I asked. Ted Hollaway is the boy she went to the formal dance with.

"Ted Hollaway?" She sounded like she'd never heard the name before. "Oh, Ted is an absolute *enfant*."

As I remember it, Beth hadn't thought so the night he asked her to the formal, but I guess when you start riding around in boys' convertibles and inboards, anyone whose father has to drive them to a dance is a mere child.

"Jimmy is much more mature," she said. She sounded like our science teacher discussing two specimens. "He really knows what's happening, if you know what I mean."

Actually I didn't have the foggiest idea what she meant, but I nodded my head anyway. Since Beth has been in the social whirl, her conversation has taken on the tone of the Woman of Experience. Only I happen to know she gets her dialogue from the magazines and the old movies we used to watch on TV. She's particularly partial to Bette Davis and Lauren Bacall movies. As far as I know she hasn't yet said to a boy, "Anytime you want me, just whistle," but only because she hasn't met the right boy yet. I have found that the best way to deal with this is to ignore it. Sooner or later she reverts back to her normal self. Now, though, I wanted to ask her an important question, and I didn't want a movie-dialogue answer.

"Did he kiss you good night?" I asked.

She finished pinning the last roller into position and then said, "*Naturellement*" in a very Bette Davisish tone. But when I looked at her she had this peculiar expression on her face, like she was trying hard not to laugh.

"What happened?" I demanded. I didn't see anything particularly funny about being kissed good night.

Beth sat down on the end of the bed with her legs dangling over the iron rail, and suddenly she looked like the old Beth again. "Oh, Kathy, you won't believe what happened. He parked the car and walked me up to the front door and, you know, it was really romantic with the moon and stars and everything and then he leaned over and kissed me, and you know what I did?"

"What?"

"I stepped on his foot."

I looked at her and she looked at me and I said, "Oh, no. You didn't," and she said, "I did," and we both started laughing. I laughed until I got a pain in my side, and Beth laughed so hard she fell over backward onto the bed and she just lay there rolling from side to side like she was in mortal pain. And I had this secret relieved feeling because Beth had done exactly the kind of thing I was scared to death I'd do. Suave Beth. *Quel* disaster!

All of a sudden I looked at Beth's travel alarm on the bureau and it said 10:03, and I felt the jumping beans back in my stomach. I wasn't even dressed yet and my hair was still in rollers.

"Beth," I said. "He's going to be here in exactly twenty-seven minutes and I am not going to be ready."

She sat right up and said, "Yes, you will." One nice thing about Beth—you can count on her when you need her. She's sort of like my mother that way. She knows how to get things done and is very efficient. She started bustling around the room making executive decisions. "Get dressed first," she said, "and then I'll comb out your hair. You can put your makeup on last."

It didn't take long to get dressed. All I had to do was put on my bathing suit, and I didn't even have to decide which one because I only have one I'd be seen in public in. It's an almost-bikini. For some weird reason my mother thinks it's obscene for a young lady to display her belly button in a bathing suit, so I had to go all over town looking for one that covered it up. The whole thing seemed pretty silly to me. After all, men's bathing suits don't cover their belly buttons, and my father's belly button has never struck me as a very sexy sight. My mother wasn't persuaded by this argument, so I finally bought this sort of modified bikini. In my case, it doesn't seem to matter very much. I don't look sexy either with or without belly-button exposure. Have you ever seen a sexy-looking concentration-camp victim? My bathing suit, by the way, is about the size of four Kleenexes and it cost $19.95. The real bikinis, which are the size of three Kleenexes, cost $25. Figure that out.

Over my bathing suit I put on a very nice see-through beach shirt that my mother made for me and I was dressed. Beth checked my rollers and they were done so she combed me out. She teased the top a little and pinned it the way they showed you in the magazine with a little blue-and-white bow, and it actually looked as nice as it did in the picture. It would have looked even nicer if I had a hairpiece, but I haven't gotten the courage yet to bring up that subject with my mother. Anyway, I guess wearing a hairpiece when you're going water-skiing might turn out to be embarrassing. Beth sprayed on about a ton of hair spray, and then I went into my parents' room and borrowed my mother's French perfume to cover up the hair-spray smell. It's *My Sin*, which always struck me as pretty funny for my mother to wear, since she's strictly the wholesome type, but it made me feel adventurous. I dabbed it on with reckless abandon, behind my ears, on my throat where the pulse is, on the insides of my wrists, and behind my knees. These are the four places recommended in an article Beth and I read in *Cosmopolitan* about using all the senses to lure a man.

At exactly 10:18 I locked myself in the bathroom with Beth's magnifying mirror and her kit of cosmetics. She has every beauty concoction known to cosmetic science even though she has this flawless complexion. I decided not to fool around with blusher or mascara or the false eyelashes Beth offered to lend me, because I knew it would all come off in a big gloppy mess as soon as I hit the water. So I just used a little eyebrow pencil and her eyelash curler and the stuff she has for covering up her nonexistent pimples for my chin. I brushed my teeth again to make sure I had kissable breath and put on lipstick and then gave myself a once-over in the mirror. I thought I looked fairly nice, but it's a funny thing—you can't really tell about yourself. I know my large blue-gray eyes are my best feature, and I have good nonbushy eyebrows and an O.K. mouth and a little too big but not really immense nose like my father's, but I can't tell what they add up to. I mean, I know I'm not gorgeous or some boy would have noticed it before now, but I'd like to know if I'm a little bit pretty. You get so used to looking at the same old face in the mirror that you can't tell. It's like looking at a wall—it's sort of neither here nor there. Every once in a while I try to catch a glimpse of myself when I don't expect it, like in a store window or something. I figure I might see myself as others see me. But it doesn't seem to work. I always recognize myself instantly and instead of thinking, "Oh, she's pretty," or "Oh, how revolting," I think, "Oh, that's me."

"How are you doing?" called Beth from the living room. "Need any help?"

"No, I'm almost ready," I called back.

Saying that made my stomach do a double flip. It was almost time. What if Keith was disappointed when he saw me in the daylight? Or what if he wasn't really as great as I remembered? Maybe he wasn't so good-looking after all, or maybe he had some terrible defect that I'd overlooked. Most likely neither of us would have a thing to say when we saw each other again. It had probably just been the moonlight that had made everything seem so perfect last night. I practiced smiling into the mirror the way I would when I saw him. It came out looking stiff and phony. I tried again. This time I looked like a circus clown. Friendly, but not too eager, that's what it should look like. Under no circumstances should the girl appear eager.

Just as my face muscles were starting to hurt from

so much smiling, I heard a light tap on the front screen door. It was only 10:25 so it couldn't be Keith. But then I heard Beth's voice saying, "Hi, you're Keith, aren't you? I'm Beth Hardy. I'm visiting Kathy for a few days."

My heart started its wild gyrations, and I wondered how I could have been so demented as to stay in the bathroom until the very last minute. I put an evil curse on the idiot who had built our cabin so that all the rooms opened off the living room. For a wild moment I found myself contemplating the bathroom window and actually seriously considering climbing out and going around to the back door so I could make a sophisticated entrance through the kitchen. But then I came to my senses. The bathroom window is next to the ceiling and is about large enough to permit the passage of an undernourished cat. Even I am not quite that thin. I also decided that I had to get a hold of myself. After all, if Beth could step on a boy's foot when he kissed her good night, I could make my grand entrance from the bathroom.

So I smiled one last rather sickly smile into the mirror, and with my hand hardly shaking at all, opened the bathroom door.

Keith was sitting in the green plaid chair by the

fireplace, which is the only comfortable chair in the cabin. He stood up, and I saw that he had on a knit shirt the exact color of his eyes, which were the most gorgeous shade of blue, and he was every bit as good-looking in the daytime as he had been last night.

"Hi, Keith," I said, and I couldn't help myself. I smiled eagerly.

Four

He had on this terrific-smelling aftershave. It smelled like limes and salt water mixed together with just the slightest hint of cloves. This may not actually sound so great, but it was very masculine and outdoorsy and seemed just right for Keith. I didn't ask him the name of it because it didn't seem like the kind of thing to ask a boy on your first real date, but I know I'll never forget the way it smelled. Years from now if I meet someone wearing that particular aftershave I'll probably go right out of my mind and chase him down the street, even if he is sixty years old and looks like a frog. This is known as a conditioned reflex. We learned about it last year in general science.

I think that's what I'll always remember about that day—the smell of his aftershave and the way the lake and the sky looked so blue they weren't quite real and, most of all, the walk home from Jimmy Weston's house. It was the longest and the shortest walk of my life. The water-skiing I'll hardly remember at all.

We did go skiing with Beth and Jimmy in the inboard with the real-leather upholstery, and Keith was a good skier, just like I predicted. Jimmy was pretty good too. The only difference between them was that Jimmy stuck to things that he knew how to do and didn't fall once, while Keith kept trying new tricks and fell about twenty times. He tried to jump the wake on one ski, which I know is hard because I always fall on my face when I try it on two. I'm not a very good water-skier; every time I try anything the slightest bit new I fall, and every time I fall I get cold waiting in the water to be picked up, and then I decide to quit. Beth had never skied before and she tried it a few times, but she never did get up so she quit too. I couldn't blame her. It gets a little embarrassing when everyone is watching and giving advice and you just keep demonstrating new and spectacular ways to fall that no one ever thought of before. It wasn't exactly Beth's most graceful hour. Jimmy was very nice about it, though. He kept trying to give her pointers while Keith ran the boat, and he didn't laugh. He was nice to Keith and me too. I decided that Beth was right. He isn't exactly shy, just sort of quiet and independent. And he doesn't have to keep showing off that he has all those boats and cars and houses and things, like a lot of people would. Keith had to ask him twice about the catamaran moored near the dock before he mentioned that it was his.

Beth had brought her camera, and she took pictures of the boys skiing and of Keith and me in the boat, and I took one of her and Jimmy on the dock. Then we had lunch sitting in wrought-iron chairs around a glass-topped table near the water. It was beautiful there, green and shady and quiet. The Westons have a real lawn that looks like a gardener takes care of it, and flowers and bushes that look as if they were planted with some plan in mind (as opposed to ours, which obviously just happened to grow there), and huge old trees with hammocks strung between them. It looked like the pictures Beth and I used to clip from *House Beautiful*. Lunch was chicken-salad-and-watercress sandwiches with the crusts cut off the bread and lemonade in an icy pitcher with mint leaves on top. It was served by a maid. I never knew before that maids existed at the lake. It was what my mother would have called the lap of luxury. But nice, not ostentatious or anything. The maid was almost invisible. My mother, on the other hand, is always very visible when she serves lunch. Her idea of lunch is ham-and-cheese or bologna or tuna-fish sandwiches, and she's even been known to stoop to peanut-butter-and-jelly. And she has never ever cut the crusts off the bread. If anyone dared suggest such a thing to her she would look at them with sincere astonishment and say, "But that's where all the vitamins are." My mother is not what you would call sophisticated.

After lunch Jimmy had to go to town to get something for the catamaran, and he asked Beth to go with him. He offered to take us too, or drop us at my house, but Keith said we'd walk home. It was already almost two o'clock.

We walked very slowly and I showed him things along the way, like the cabin we used to rent when I was very small and the beach where I learned to swim and the high dive that I jumped off once when Patsy Regan bet me a Peter Paul Almond Joy that I wouldn't do it. It was probably the most terrifying moment of my entire life, and I resolved never to do it again, a resolution which has been easy to keep. We walked in the road with our fingertips just touching, and the asphalt was hot through the soles of my sneakers. Once a car went by and we had to move out of the road and it was the Olivers. I waved to them casually as if I always walked along the road holding hands with a boy like this. Mrs. Oliver waved back with a big beaming smile, and I felt a little giddy, like the time I had a glass of champagne at a wedding.

When we came to the dirt road that leads to Lone Point, Keith asked, "Where does that go?"

I looked at him out of the corner of my eye to see if he really didn't know or if someone had told him it was a famous lovers' lane and he had been planning all along to lure me there.

I couldn't tell, but he wasn't leering or drooling or anything, so I told him the story about the Parsons family who owned the point and how they had built this big beautiful house about eight or ten years ago. Then the first summer they moved in there was a canoeing accident and their five-year-old daughter was drowned and they went away and never came back. "They still own the point," I finished, "and a caretaker comes and looks at it every once in a while. But no one has lived there since then."

"Sounds like a haunted house," said Keith. "Let's go take a look." He started down the road, pulling my hand. I hesitated, not knowing if I should go, but then I knew that I really wanted to go there with Keith even if it was a lovers' lane. Or maybe because it was. I wanted to remember being there with him. Anyway, boys didn't attack you in broad daylight, I was pretty sure. It was parked cars and drive-in movies that you had to watch out for.

Keith looked at me and said with kind of half a smile, "It's all right. I'm really harmless," and I could feel my face turning twelve shades of purple because he'd read my mind.

"Oh, I just wondered if there was time," I said. "Won't they be waiting for you to go back to camp?"

"Let them wait," he said, and squeezed my hand.

The road was narrow and choked with weeds, but you could tell cars had been there because there was grease on the tops of the tall grass between the two tire tracks. I walked in one track and he walked in the other, and he held my hand up so it wouldn't brush against the greasy grass. It was cool and shady and there were bugs hovering over the low places in the road which were full of the last rain, and they buzzed in our ears and made Keith slap his neck. The woods seemed to be reaching out from either side to swallow the road, and maybe they would in another few years. It smelled like damp and pine needles and grass.

Near the point the woods changed to tall pine trees crowded close together with bare gray trunks, and you could see the lake through them on either side. In the middle of the point, facing a cove with pine trees all around it like guards, was a big, square, used-to-be white house, all shuttered up so it looked asleep. It made you want to walk on tiptoe so as not to disturb it. We walked around the house, talking in a whisper, and on the front porch Keith found a shutter that was off its hinge and we peered inside.

I expected to see a bunch of old wicker furniture like ours, covered up with sheets and all cobwebby, but instead it looked like a living room you would see in one of the home-decoration magazines. Dusty, of course, since it wasn't covered with sheets, but all antique-type furniture—French Provincial or Queen Anne or one of those styles.

Pressing my forehead against the glass so as to eliminate the reflections of the trees, I could make out a couple of tall wing chairs and a striped couch with skinny legs that didn't look safe to sit down on and a desk like my mother's that she calls a secretary. There were huge, glassed-in bookcases made of carved wood and paintings in gold frames and tied-back drapes of faded dark-red velvet. But the really creepy thing was the vase of flowers on the coffee table. They must have been fake but they looked real. It looked like the family had just left a few minutes ago to go shopping in town.

Keith must have been thinking the same thing because he whistled under his breath and said, "You mean it's been like this for ten years?"

All of a sudden I felt embarrassed to be looking, like we were reading someone else's mail or something. I looked at Keith and he seemed to know what I meant, and he closed the shutter again carefully so no one could see it was broken.

We walked along the little beach in front of the

house, and I had this weird feeling that someone was watching us from behind the shutters, like maybe the Parsons family hadn't really gone away at all. And at the same time I felt good because I'd done something with Keith that I'd never done with anyone else and I knew I'd remember it.

He leaned over and picked up a flat white pebble and skipped it into the lake, and without thinking about it I skipped one too. His skipped three times and then sank, and mine skipped four.

"Hey, you've got a good arm. We could use you on our basketball team," he said, and then I remembered that under no circumstances whatever is the girl supposed to beat the boy in any athletic endeavor. Like even if you're an Olympic swimmer, you're supposed to take little dinky strokes and squeal a lot and pretend you can't quite make it to the raft. You have to make them think they are big and strong at all times. It's got something to do with their masculine virility.

But the funny thing was that suddenly I didn't care. "It just so happens," I said, "that my father holds the world stone-skipping record of nine skips. And he taught me all I know."

"That so?" said Keith. "I should have known better than to tangle with you." He didn't seem to care either. And I couldn't detect any slipping of his masculine virility.

Everything after that was like a dream. I showed him the little summerhouse that the Parsons had built on the very tip of Lone Point. It's round and made of stone, like a fort with open sides and two little benches inside made out of birch logs. The benches are too rickety to sit down on now, and the whole thing is in the process of crumbling, but it's beautiful anyway because of where it is. Lone Point sticks way out into the lake, so you feel like you're on an island away from everything, and you can see up and down the lake for miles. I had this funny feeling that I could see things better than I ever had before, like I was wearing some kind of magical glasses that made everything brighter and closer and clearer. The lake and sky had never seemed so blue to me, and I could make out every tree on the other shore, each one separate and distinct like a bright green cutout.

We climbed out on a rock and I took off my sneakers without even thinking of the hideousness of my feet and dangled my toes in the clear water. We watched the waves from some passing boat come nearer and nearer until they lapped with little licking sounds over the rocks that went out in a line to a red-and-white marker. The air smelled of grass and some kind of wild flowers mixed with Keith's aftershave, and the whole world seemed to be painted blue and green except for the white triangles of sailboats in a race down the lake and the red roof of a house on the next point and the red-and-white marker. I wished suddenly that the day would never end.

Keith put his hand over mine on the rock, and I looked down and noticed his hands for the first time. They were just like I'd thought they would be—square and strong and brown with a few dark hairs growing on the tops of his fingers.

He asked me about school then and I told him that my best subject was English and my worst was math, and it turned out that he hated math too. And we both liked ancient history, and he was a terrible speller and had flunked eighth-grade English. That was when his parents decided to send him to private school, so he could get into college. He didn't know if he wanted to go to college or not, though, because music was his thing. He played the guitar and sang and had written a couple of his own songs, and if it turned out he couldn't make it as a singer or a song writer he was going to be a disk jockey and maybe own his own radio station someday. He told me all about his guitar, which he'd saved up for over a year and bought with his own money and which was the only thing he had that he'd care about rescuing if the house caught on fire or something. "My mother would stand around wringing her hands about her English bone china and her real antique spinning wheel and her ten-speed blender, but I'd just save my guitar and let everything else go up in smoke," he said.

There are three different kinds of guitars, he explained to me. Classical, folk, and country and western. He has a country and western. It has a better sound than a folk guitar—deeper resonance. He never took any lessons; he taught himself to play by listening to records. He didn't bring his good guitar to camp with him because of the dampness being bad for the wood, and besides, he didn't want to take the chance of some dumb kid stepping on it. Instead he brought an old one with a crack in it.

I asked him who his favorite singers were and they were mostly names I'd never heard of, the real country singers who aren't well known but who really started the sound that the big names made famous. And he had all the albums the Beatles ever made. It turned out that "Yesterday," my favorite Beatles song of all time, was one of his favorites too, and that made it our song.

He sang a little bit of it for me, looking out over the water, and the words were sad and made me think about his leaving. He had a nice voice, soft and husky but right on tune. I watched his face while he was singing and saw how his hair curled over the edge of his collar in back and how the sunlight made it glint red where it fell over his forehead. He was frowning a little bit in concentration and his profile looked like one of those old Romans you see on coins. I was trying to take a picture of that moment with my mind so I'd have it for later, after he'd gone.

He stopped singing and looked at me, and my heart started beating a zillion times a minute because I knew for sure this time that he was going to kiss me. He leaned toward me and I took a deep breath like I was about to jump off the high dive and then suddenly, for no reason at all, I pointed down the lake and said, "Isn't that Beth and Jimmy out there?"

He gave me a funny look and then glanced where I was pointing, but the sailboat was too far away to see who was in it for sure. And I was thinking what an idiot I was and what was I afraid of anyway? Maybe I was scared that I'd do something to spoil the moment like Beth had or that it wouldn't be perfect like everything else or something. I sat very still hoping he'd lean toward me again, but the moment was past and I'd blown my chance.

He stood up and reached down his hand to me and pulled me up. "The guys are probably sending out search parties all over the place," he said. "I better get you home."

So we walked back down the dirt road, not hurrying even though it had to be past three o'clock by now. When we were almost to my house we saw the two boys who had been with Keith last night heading down the road to the beach.

"Hey, Bradley," called the taller one, who had red hair. "The stuff's in the canoes and everyone's waiting for you. Don's really teed off."

"Be there in five minutes," Keith called back, not looking at all upset. "Tell him to cool it."

But he didn't walk any faster. I looked back and saw the two boys just standing in the road staring at us, and for the first time in my life I felt like some sort of *femme fatale*. Like Helen of Troy preventing the fleet from sailing or something.

When we got to the cabin there was no one there, and we stood by the front steps just like last night, holding hands and not saying much but not wanting to say good-bye. And all I was thinking really was that if he left without kissing me I would positively die, and I hardly paid any attention to what he was saying. Then he was asking if he could write to me, and of course I said yes, and then I had to go inside and get a piece of paper so we could both write our addresses on it. He was leaving camp the next weekend and would be home for a couple of weeks before school started.

"Maybe you could come up for a weekend in the fall," he said. "For a football game or a track meet or something."

"That would be fun," I said, trying not to sound too eager, when what I really wanted to do was make him promise he meant it and wasn't just being polite and suggest that we set a definite date right this minute.

He carefully ripped the paper with our addresses on it in half and folded his half and put it in the pocket of his shirt and handed the other half to me.

"Well, I better be going before they shove off without me," he said, and I didn't answer because I was saying *kiss me* so loud inside that I was afraid if I opened my mouth I'd shout it. And then, just as if he'd received my thought waves, he leaned toward me, and

(71

it was like a slow-motion movie as his face came closer and closer and I saw him close his eyes and then at the last second I closed mine and he kissed me. It was a nice kiss, soft and gentle but not too much so, like we were related or something, and not wet and sloppy either, like I remembered from playing post office at Mary Lou Dawson's birthday party once a long time ago. And we didn't bump noses or anything like that.

Then it was over. I opened my eyes and he was smiling at me.

"Well, so long, Kathy," he said. "Don't forget to write now."

"You either," I said. "Bye."

He reached out and touched a piece of hair that had fallen in my eyes and pushed it back and said, "Be good." And then he turned and walked down the path.

I couldn't stand to watch him walk away so I went slowly up the steps to the porch; not looking back but with the touch of his hand forever on my problem hair.

Five

I was lying on my back on my purple-and-orange striped beach towel next to Beth's with the black-and-white STOP sign on it. We had just turned over, a ritual which we performed religiously every half hour in order to insure getting golden gloriously bronze all over.

"Is my nose starting to burn?" asked Beth.

I made the large sacrifice of turning my head toward her and opening my eyes. I had been making it a point to open them as seldom as possible on the beach because I wasn't wearing my sunglasses. I have firmly resolved this year not to end up with a ghastly untanned mask around my eyes where my glasses were. This is what happened last year and Beth called me Owl Eyes for the entire month of September.

"No, your nose isn't starting to burn," I told her. "How could it with that ton of white gook you've got on it?"

"Well, I'll just die if it peels again. It's peeled four times already and it looks positively *gauche*."

This is quite a record, I must admit, inasmuch as Beth has only been at the lake a little over a week. But she has very tender skin. Burn and peel, burn and peel, that's all it knows how to do. I, on the other hand, have gradually been turning golden gloriously bronze and will soon be the absolute image of those models you see in the magazines posing acrobatically with windswept hair on beaches with names like St. Tropez and Ibiza and Torremolinos. Getting a tan is the one beauty problem I don't have. The sun is even doing wonders for my oily skin. About the only problem area I have left is my chin, which is probably one of our nation's great remaining natural resources for oil.

"What time is it?" I asked Beth.

She brought her left wrist up to her eyes in a languorous Lauren Bacall motion and said, "It's only quarter of two. Honestly, Kathy, that's the fifth time you've asked me in the last half hour. You've got another whole hour to go."

Three o'clock is the magic hour when the mail comes in at the store. It only comes in once a day, and I never took the slightest interest in it in the past because I never got any. Maybe one letter from Beth in the three weeks we were here or a note from my grandmother with a dollar in it or something. It was never a big thing in my life. But all of a sudden it has taken on great vital importance. One reason for this, of course, is that I'm hoping for a letter from Keith. I know it's really too soon because it hasn't even been a whole week since he was here and he's not home from camp yet, but I can't help secretly hoping anyway. The other reason is that Beth and I are waiting for the pictures she took of the four of us water-skiing. She sent them to some photography place to be developed.

(75

I can understand how my newfound devotion to the mailbox might get on Beth's nerves. I think it's also beginning to get on the nerves of the little old lady at the store who sorts the mail and puts it into the boxes with painstaking care and deliberation while I stand there panting and trying not to appear too eager. I'm not sure what she thinks I'm expecting—probably a certified check for a million dollars. To be absolutely truthful, this mail fixation is beginning to get on *my* nerves too. Life was a lot more serene when I knew that the only person who might write to me was my grandmother.

The reason I was so anxious to get the water-skiing pictures back was because a strange thing had happened. I had totally forgotten what Keith looked like. Well, not really totally. I could remember little pieces of him, like the way his shirt touched the back of his neck and the way the dark hair grew on the tops of his fingers. But when I closed my eyes and tried to see him in my mind, there was just a big blank. I couldn't put the pieces together. The whole thing was beginning to seem like a dream that had never really happened.

Once, when I was about nine or ten, a weird thing happened to me. We had been visiting my cousins and playing hide-and-seek in their backyard, and on the way home I fell asleep in the car. When we got home I said something to Lisa about when I climbed the fence and hid in this really great hiding place, a kind of cave inside a lilac bush next door to my cousins' house. She said I didn't because we weren't allowed in the neighbor's yard and I said I did too. We got into a big fight about it and finally my mother sent me upstairs because I called Lisa a liar. But the funny thing was that I never was sure if I did climb that fence and hide inside the lilac bush or if I just dreamed I did. I can remember the rough splintery feeling of the rail fence and the way each lilac flower was really made up of hundreds of little flowers and the sweet smell of them all around me, but I could have dreamed all that or it could have happened some other time. To this day I'm not sure. It's the weirdest thing.

I felt almost the same way about Keith. I had to keep dropping his name into the conversation to make sure he was real and it had happened. I did this an average of about ninety-five times a day with Beth.

Like now I said, "Don't you think Ray looks a little like Keith around the mouth?"

Ray is the lifeguard at our beach. He also happens to be the most conceited boy who ever lived. He sits like a king on his high white chair with his transistor radio and a pair of wraparound shades covering most of his face, and he refuses to acknowledge the existence of anyone who doesn't look like Miss Universe. To my knowledge, he has never rescued anyone from drowning. I'm not even sure he knows how to swim, since I've never actually seen him immersed in water. He just lounges in his chair listening to rock music, and if anyone swims out too far he toots his whistle a couple of times and jerks his thumb at them to come in. He does happen to have broad shoulders, a Greek-god profile, and a gorgeous tan, and Beth had a minor crush on him the first couple of days she was here, until I pointed out to her his vital flaws. Like the fact that he obviously acquired his muscles lifting weights, since no one has ever seen him engaging in any kind of physical exertion in his life. Plus I have some dire suspicions about his intellect based on his vocabulary, which seems to consist entirely of "all *right*" and "out of sight, man," delivered with varying inflections to suit the occasion. And there is the revealing fact that although all the little kids follow him around with their mouths hanging open under the delusion that he is some kind of hero, he never says a single word to them. Not one. I feel that this says something about a person. Beth thought it over for a day, during which I noticed that she passed unnecessarily close to the lifeguard stand three times, with no reaction from Ray. Then she said she had to agree with me.

Now she cast him a discreet glance from under the brim of the floppy pink hat she was wearing to give additional protection to her fragile nose. "He might look a tiny bit like him around the earlobes," she said, "but that's all. Keith is much cuter."

This was exactly what I was hoping she'd say. "Well," I said, "maybe Keith looks more like Paul Newman around the mouth."

"Mmmm," said Beth, obviously not really turned on by the subject. She proceeded to change it to one of more crucial importance—what she should wear tomorrow night when Jimmy took her to the drive-in. Should she wear the green-striped shift that made her hips look like battleships or the navy bell-bottoms she'd worn with him twice already?

I considered this knotty problem. "I'd wear the shift," I advised her finally. "I got the definite impression from Keith that boys get tired of girls wearing slacks all the time."

Beth thought it over for a minute and then announced that she was going to wear the bell-bottoms.

(79

"I think I've gained five pounds since the last time I wore the shift." She raised her wrist to her eyes again. "Oops, time to turn over again."

It was always a relief to turn onto my stomach and no longer feel as if my eyeballs were on fire. I liked the feeling of the sun on my shoulders and the backs of my legs and my toes digging into the sand and the rough, soft towel under my cheek. It was almost enough to put me to sleep. I was just on the verge of dropping off when a picture floated into my mind of Keith and me sitting on the rock at Lone Point. But when I tried to zoom in on it, like with a movie camera, I still couldn't see his face. It was maddening. It was bad enough to have to listen to Beth casually discussing what she was going to wear when she saw Jimmy tomorrow night, when I might possibly see Keith in October or I might possibly never see him again in my life. But not even to be able to remember what he looked like! It wasn't fair.

Before, when I had never had a date with a boy, I used to think everything would be perfect if I could just once go out with a boy like Keith. But I never really thought past that one date, as if life would stop right there. It had never occurred to me that there could be all these other complications, like would he really write, and was he really as nice as I thought, and did he really like me or was I just a girl who happened to be around and I was all right for the weekend? And would I ever see him again?

I had this sudden conviction that I wouldn't. Have you ever noticed how in the movies great romances never last? Something always comes between them, like she turns out to have some slowly fatal disease or is already married or he has to go off to be a bomber pilot in the Pacific or has amnesia or something. I always cry a lot in this kind of movie. Take *Romeo and Juliet* as a basic example, or *Gone With the Wind* (during which I used up fourteen Kleenexes and emerged looking like I had an acute case of hay fever), or any one of a hundred Bette Davis movies on TV. I have a theory about these romances. I think they are just too beautiful to last. They're kind of like the exotic butterflies in the illustrated bug book that my grandmother once gave me for Christmas—they only live for a few short hours. I think they have to come to a tragic end because they are too beautiful to wind up in a split-level house playing bridge and doing the dishes and mowing the lawn.

My father actually enjoys mowing the lawn, which pretty well sums up why he and my mother could

(*81*

never have had the romance of the century. Neither of them has a wild, reckless bone in their bodies. Most parents I know are like that. They seem to place more value on comfort than anything else. I don't think they would want to give up everything and take the chance of being either very happy or very sad. This may explain why there don't seem to be very many great romances in real life. The only one I can think of is Beth's Aunt Elizabeth, who never got married because her one true love was a divorced man and her religious beliefs wouldn't allow her to marry him. She's about fifty years old now and takes care of her elderly mother and goes on cruises every winter and has these beautiful melancholy eyes. On her dressing table in a silver frame is a faded photograph of her true love, whose name was Douglas. He's very distinguished-looking and has sad eyes also. I think he finally moved away to some place like Oregon and got married to someone else. So she has nothing left now but her memories. I could see myself like her in about twenty years, standing at the rail of a ship gazing out to sea, left with nothing but my memories of Keith.

Then I had a really depressing thought. What if the pictures Beth took didn't come out? I could be left without even a photograph for my dressing table.

"Beth," I said. "What time is it now?"

She flung out her wrist in my general direction.

"I'm going to start up," I decided. "Are you coming or not?"

"What time is it?" she mumbled from under her hat.

"Twenty-five of."

"Oh, all right." She sat up and removed her hat, blinking at the sun. "Between your mother's rule about an hour after lunch and your three-o'clock date with the mailbox, I may never swim again."

Beth swims about an average of three minutes a week unless there's a major heat wave, so I couldn't feel too sorry for her.

She started fishing around in her beach bag for her mirror.

"Come on," I said. "You don't have to give yourself a complete face-lift just to go to the store."

"Looking your best is a twenty-four-hour-a-day job," Beth said, quoting from a magazine article we'd read that morning. "And anyway, you never can tell who you'll meet at the mailbox."

"Well, it won't be Jimmy," I pointed out. "Unless he decided to come back by jet." He had driven his mother to Vermont to pick up his sister at Camp Wichiwachee, which happens to be a very exclusive camp for overweight girls interested in learning foreign languages. Jimmy didn't tell us about the overweight part; I read it in an ad in the back of a travel magazine.

Beth shrugged and continued to study her damaged nose in the mirror. I had to admit that in my heart I knew she was right in her attitude toward beauty. I will probably never have the face and body beautiful they're always talking about in the magazines because I'm just not devoted enough to make it a twenty-four-hour-a-day job.

While she was flicking a hairbrush lightly over her bangs, I walked over to where my mother was sitting on a blanket talking to Mrs. Oliver and asked her to watch our stuff while we were gone. My mother gave me that secret smile she's been using lately to indicate she's aware of what I'm up to, but mercifully said nothing.

As I walked back I happened to look across the lake and something red caught my eye. It was a tree that had just started to turn. And just like that I knew the summer was over. It happens every year. You go along and summer seems like a permanent thing, a long, luxurious, slow, sleepy time, and then suddenly one day there's a chill when you get up in the morning, a different smell in the air, a dry leaf drifting down from a tree, and—bang—summer is gone. It always makes me sad. But then, the end of anything makes me sad, even things any normal person would be glad were over. When I'm older I'll probably become disgustingly sentimental like my grandmother.

We walked up the road, Beth poking along and me about six steps ahead of her. Beth was practicing walking gracefully like models do, placing one foot directly in front of the other and sort of gliding along. Whenever I try it, I trip over my size-10 sneakers. She also found it necessary to stop every two steps to pick up a pine cone or remove a pebble from her sandal or something. Walking with Beth is like the hare taking a stroll with the tortoise. Hurrying is against her principles. I have never seen her walk briskly in my life. She grudgingly accelerates to a trot when we have to run the fifty-yard dash in gym class, but that's her top speed. We have been late for school countless times because of her. In the sixth grade it got so bad that the principal called our mothers in for a conference, and for about a week after that, my mother wouldn't let me wait for Beth on the corner.

I was attempting to carry on a conversation with her over my shoulder, which can get pretty trying. I was explaining Keith's theory about the influence of the great composers of the Baroque period on the music of the Beatles. As we passed the tennis courts I said, "He feels that the contrapuntal rhythms of Bach and Vivaldi were very important." I looked back to see if she understood and she wasn't even there. She had stopped to watch a tennis match and hadn't heard a word I said.

Anyway, we finally got to the store at five of three. Beth stopped outside to weigh herself on the penny scale on the porch, which was the real reason she came with me.

"I knew it," she said with a pained look when the needle finally came to rest. "I should never have let Jimmy take me to that pizza place. *Tres mauvais!*" Pizza is Beth's other fatal weakness.

Beth had another penny, so I weighed myself too. As usual, I weighed exactly ninety-eight pounds.

While Beth was making new resolutions about total abstinence from food I went inside. I looked in our mailbox, and naturally there was nothing in it. But I could see the back of the mail lady's blue dress, and I could tell she had started sorting. Beth wandered in to look in the gift shop while I stood watch at the box. The store, which is known by the original name of Hank's Store, has a little bit of everything—basic groceries, a soda fountain, paperbacks, little pine-filled pillows that say *Adirondack Mts., New York* on them, candy bars, suntan lotion, magazines, and gifts. Beth has been carefully studying the selection of gifts ever since she got here, trying to decide on a hostess present for my mother.

I watched the mail lady going through her routine with her customary maddening slowness—my mother says she has arthritis but I personally was convinced she did it to drive me up the wall—and I decided that this was absolutely the last day I was going to pick up the mail. It was too hard on my nerves. From now on I would just wait until my father got around to stopping for it, which is usually after supper. Anyway, a watched mailbox never has a letter in it, as Beth has been telling me for the last week. I think she is right. As long as I'm waiting for it and expecting it and counting on it I'll never get a letter from Keith.

Just as I was thinking that, my mother's words popped into my mind again: "A girl in every port." I felt an instant depression setting in because I'd been trying not to think of them. She said them to my father late last night when she thought I was asleep. (You don't say anything confidential in our cabin unless you're pretty sure people are asleep, on account of the walls being made of cardboard.) I wasn't listening to the first part of the conversation because I didn't know it was going to be about me, but then I heard my mother say, "I hope she won't be too upset if she doesn't hear from him. I'm awfully afraid he may be the kind who has a girl in every port." There was a silence and then some newspaper rustling and my father said, "Oh, I don't know, he seemed sincere enough. He lives a long way off, though. Didn't she say he goes to school in New Hampshire?" All day long the words had been playing themselves over and over in my brain like a stuck record: "A girl in every port. . . . He lives a long way off." I didn't want to think about it because I was afraid if I did I'd know they were both right. Why should he bother with a girl who lived so far away? Most likely there was a girls' school right next door to the boys' school where he went and dozens of girls with flawless complexions and hair that gleamed who were dying to go out with him, and all he had to do was pick up the phone and he could get a date with anyone he wanted. There was one advantage to going out with a creep that I hadn't thought of before. You wouldn't have to worry about the competition from other girls. Unfortunately that was the only advantage.

The mail lady turned around and started putting little handfuls of letters in the boxes. She always started at the top and our box was in the third row down. When she got to the second row she suddenly looked right out through an empty mailbox and our eyes met. It was just like in the movies—she gave me this hypnotic stare with her watery blue eyes and I was powerless to look away. Then she smiled ever so slightly in a knowing way, just like my mother in fact. That broke the spell and I managed to look away and then pretended to yawn from the boredom of having to pick up the mail. And then she put about four letters and a gray envelope into our box.

I forced myself to take my time dialing the combination, like I couldn't care less. Twice to the right to A, then left to K, then to 124. The minute I saw the gray envelope I knew it was the pictures. It was fat and addressed to Beth. I flipped through the letters but I could tell at a glance they were all for my parents. A note from my grandmother, a postcard with a picture of a lake on it like they're always getting from their friends, a letter from an insurance company, and a bill from some department store.

I ran to the gift shop and waved the gray envelope under Beth's nose. "They're here!" I announced.

She was examining a set of little cut-glass vials and didn't even look up. "Do you think your mother would like these?" she asked.

"What are they?"

"Vinegar-and-oil cruets, of course."

"Beth, you know my mother serves only Thousand Island dressing from the store. Come on, it's the pictures."

She gave the cruets one last appraising look and followed me outside.

We sat down on the stone wall in front of the store and I shoved the envelope in her hand. She looked at it, felt it, and turned it over. I thought she was going to take its pulse. "Hurry up, open it," I said, fighting an overpowering urge to grab it and rip it open myself. She started slitting open the top with about as much painstaking care as the mail lady. I wondered if they were secretly related or something.

Finally she got it open and pulled out a pile of prints. I leaned over her shoulder to see. Right on top was this truly horrendous picture of me lying on my beach towel with my limp hair and my toothpick shape squinting into the sun. One more of my beauty problems which I may not have mentioned is that I take terrible pictures. I always look as if I'm sneering for some reason. Whether I try to look sultry *à la* Lauren Bacall or slightly mysterious in the style of the Mona Lisa or even if I'm not trying to look like anything in particular, it always comes out as a sneer. It's very discouraging.

The next one was of Beth completely hidden by her pink hat. Another winner. Then there was a stunning shot of our cabin. And a thrilling view of the lake as seen from our front porch. And my father driving the boat. I have never seen so many boring pictures in all my life. They all came out perfectly too, since they were of such boring subjects. I kept grabbing them out of Beth's hand in case she had any ideas about spending a half hour studying each one. We had just about reached the bottom of the pile, and I was convinced that the water-skiing ones hadn't come out at all, when there they were.

There were four of them. The first was of Keith jumping the wake on one ski, taken from so far away that if you hadn't known who it was, you'd never have known who it was. You know the kind—a real waste of film. Next was one of Jimmy driving the boat. It was a little out of focus but not too bad. And then there was Keith sitting behind the steering wheel with me beside him and his arm around me behind the red leather seat. I grabbed it.

There he was, big and tan and muscular-looking in the blue shirt and smiling that supergreat smile. He was gorgeous. And next to him I looked almost small, and my hair wasn't in too hideous disarray and I was smiling and, miracle of miracles, it didn't look like a sneer.

"Oh, Beth, it's perfect!" I said.

She was busy looking at the last picture, and I tore myself away from the one of Keith and me to look. It was the shot I'd taken of her and Jimmy standing on the dock. He looked like he wasn't quite sure what to do with his hands, and his head was turned at a funny angle and his ears stuck out, but it was cute.

"This one's good too," I said.

Beth was frowning. "I knew I never should have worn that bathing suit," she said. But she liked the picture, I could tell.

Then she looked at the one of Keith and me and said I looked positively *suave* and maybe Keith did resemble Paul Newman a little around the mouth after all and did I want her to order a five-by-seven enlargement from the photography place on their special summer discount so I could have one to frame and one for my wallet. I said yes, naturally.

I couldn't stop looking at the picture, it was so perfect. And now that I had it, it all came back to me and I could remember exactly how he looked. It was amazing. I was so engrossed in analyzing every little nuance of his expression that the letters for my parents slid off my lap without my noticing, and when I leaned over to pick them up the postcard had turned over and there, staring up at me, was my name written in big sprawling handwriting that I'd never seen before.

Suddenly the world seemed to come to an abrupt stop. I stared at the card in a trance, then looked over at the message side. It was signed "Love, Keith."

Love, Keith.

My stomach turned inside out.

"What is it?" asked Beth.

I opened my mouth and made some incoherent gurgling sound.

"From him?"

I nodded, being incapable of human speech. Clutching the card like it really was a check for a million dollars, I climbed back on the wall and pushed the hair out of my eyes, taking my time to hold onto the moment even though my heart was suddenly thumping away at a rate of about five hundred beats a minute.

And then I read:

Hi, Kathy—
Today was Camper's Day—a bad scene for counsellers.
I got dumped in the lake so many times I may never
dry out. Those guys in the senior bunk are rough
characters. We beat them in the canue race, though.
Tomorrow we break down the tents and the next day
head for home. Am writing a new song in honor of last
weekend and hope to try it out on you soon.

Love,
Keith

I turned the card over. On the back was a picture
of a bright blue lake with rocks and pine trees and
two people water-skiing. Very scenic. I turned back
to the message side and read the small print on top. It
said: "Hemlock Lake in the scenic northern Adiron-
dacks. Known for its clear water, numerous hiking
trails, and excellent fishing, this is a favorite vacation
and camping spot." Then I read what Keith had
written all over again, slower this time. I noticed that
his handwriting was kind of messy, almost like a third
grader, and that he'd spelled *counselor* wrong and also
canoe. How could anyone not know how to spell
canoe? But it didn't matter. It was what he'd said that
counted.

(94

"What did he say?" asked Beth.

I handed her the card. She read it and handed it back with that same sly Cheshire-cat grin that everybody seemed to be giving me lately.

"What do you think?"

"*C'est magnifique!*"

"What does he mean about trying out his new song on me soon?"

"*C'est facile.* He's obviously going to invite you up for a football weekend."

"Do you really think so?"

"*Certainement.*"

Suddenly I felt like I was going to simply explode with happiness. Usually I don't show much how I feel, being what my mother calls self-contained, but sitting there with Keith's picture in one hand and his postcard in the other, my container just burst.

"Can you imagine," I said to Beth, "being the subject of a song? I wonder what he'll call it. I can't wait to hear it. After he invites me up there, I could invite him to visit me, couldn't I? I mean for a dance at school or something. Maybe at Christmas. They probably have a long Christmas vacation at private school. Oh, I wish I'd brought some money with me. I want to buy one of those frames in the gift shop."

I went on like this for a few minutes and Beth got sort of excited too in spite of herself, and we decided to go back inside the store and look at the picture frames. They had these plastic ones in all different colors with a heart shape cut out for the picture. A turquoise-blue one or maybe a yellow one would go with my room at home and it would be just right for the picture of Keith and me.

Just as we were about to go in the door, Tommy Whitaker and a friend of his named Sandy something-or-other came out. I'd seen Sandy a few times but he was quiet and sort of nondescript—the kind of boy that you never really remember. This time, though, I noticed that he was taller than me and that he'd gotten new horn-rimmed glasses that made him look much more interesting. Sort of intellectual. Not like Keith, of course, but interesting.

"Hi, girls," Tommy said. He had a *Playboy* magazine rolled up under his arm. "Last basketball game tonight." Then he turned to me with a big grin and said, "Hey, is your camper friend going to be around this weekend? We could use another tall guy."

It was the first time Tommy Whitaker had spoken to me all summer. I could feel myself turning pink, but I felt so good I couldn't care less. "No, he's back at camp," I said. "On Hemlock Lake."

"Too bad. Well, are you girls going to come and cheer us on anyway?"

"We might," said Beth the Supercool.

"If you promise not to land in my lap," I added.

"But that's the best part of the game," Tommy protested. "You don't want me to have any fun."

"His lap aim has always been better than his basket aim," Sandy said seriously.

I laughed, and Tommy said they'd see us later and they walked away.

As we went up the stairs to the store that laugh rang in my ears. There was something familiar about it; I seemed to have heard it somewhere before. And then I remembered.

It bore a slight but very distinct resemblance to Lisa's famous giggle.

So that is the story of how my life changed overnight and I became a new summer me, like they said in the magazine article.

I now have Keith's picture in my wallet and a five-by-seven enlargement in the turquoise frame on my bureau, and everyone thinks he is gorgeous. Lisa is desperately jealous. A boy named Wally who works at the gas station where she and her friends are always hanging around getting air in their bike tires asked her out, but my mother wouldn't let her go. She said under no circumstances was any daughter of hers risking her life riding around town on some boy's motorcycle. What she didn't mention was that Wally is a high-school dropout who wears a leather jacket all year round, has greasy hair and a generally dangerous appearance, and she wouldn't let Lisa go to a Sunday-school picnic with him. Lisa has been sulking for days. My mother is beginning to look harried. I think she thinks it is going to be a strain having two teen-age daughters.

My main interest in life right now is our chubby balding, sixty-year-old mailman. Beth is annoyed because she says I never want to go anywhere anymore. I always have to rush home after school and check the mailbox. So far, besides the postcard, I have received one letter from Keith and I have written him one. His was two pages on both sides and contained about twelve spelling errors. It told all about track and the rock group he is forming with three other guys on his corridor and how he has to study all the time in order to pass algebra. It sounded like maybe he was too busy to have many dates. He signed it "With love." My reply took me three study halls and four nights to compose and was very gay and witty. I told him about some funny things that happened in school and about the rock concert I went to two weeks ago. I didn't mention that I went to it with Beth. After a lengthy consultation on the telephone with Beth, I signed the letter "As ever." The girl should never appear too eager.

I'm actually going to see Keith in just four more weeks. He invited me up for their big football weekend the week before Thanksgiving. When I first asked my parents they seemed pretty dubious. I could see them sending signals to each other with their eyes. I think they were worried about co-ed dorms. But after I assured them that all the boys were moving out of one dorm and turning it over to their dates and that there would be chaperons all over the place, and I promised not to breathe, practically, the whole time I was there, they said I could go. My mother is even letting me buy a new long dress for the occasion. Beth and I are going shopping for it this Saturday. She made it clear, though, that it will not have a bare midriff. Which is probably just as well because all my ribs would show.

The funny thing is that even though in some ways

my life has changed drastically, in other ways it really hasn't changed at all. School is still depressingly the same. I thought maybe things would be different this year because I was different. But the boys obviously don't realize that they're looking at a new me, and I have not been bombarded with offers of dates. The only boy who has gone out of his way to speak to me is Freddy Lipton, who treated me to a fascinating statistical analysis of the World Series. Unfortunately he was not transformed into a prince over the summer. Neither were any of the other boys in my classes, though some of them seem a little bit taller.

My plans for this Saturday night are to watch a Katherine Hepburn–Spencer Tracy movie on TV. By myself. Ted Hollaway asked Beth to the movies and she is going. She says after Jimmy he is dull and immature, but she is going.

Most discouraging of all, the new me still has the same old beauty problems. I was not magically transformed overnight into a beautiful swan. My problem skin did not miraculously disappear. I did not suddenly develop a 36-D bust. My split ends remain split. And I still bite my nails in times of stress.

There is one hopeful sign though. Yesterday in

school we were weighed and measured, and I've finally broken the 100-pound barrier. I nearly fainted when I saw it on the nurse's official scale. I now weigh 102.

I figure this may be significant.

MS READ-a-thon— a simple way to start youngsters reading

Boys and girls between 6 and 14 can join the MS READ-a-thon and help find a cure for Multiple Sclerosis by reading books. And they get two rewards — the enjoyment of reading, and the great feeling that comes from helping others.

Parents and educators: For complete information call your local MS chapter. Or mail the coupon below.

Kids can help, too!

Mail to:
National Multiple Sclerosis Society
205 East 42nd Street
New York, N.Y. 10017
I would like more information about the MS READ-a-thon and how it can work in my area.

MS Mystery Sleuth ™

Name _____
(please print)
Address_____
City_____ State_____ Zip _____
Organization_____

1—80